NOTES FROM HARD DRIVE

National Library of Canada Cataloguing in Publication Data

Jordan, Mark
Notes from hard drive / Mark Jordan.
ISBN 1-4120-0531-0
I. Title.
PS3610.O663N68 2003 813'.6 C2003-903346-5

TRAFFORD

This book was published *on-demand* in cooperation with Trafford Publishing.
On-demand publishing is a unique process and service of making a book available for retail sale to the public taking advantage of on-demand manufacturing and Internet marketing. **On-demand publishing** includes promotions, retail sales, manufacturing, order fulfilment, accounting and collecting royalties on behalf of the author.

Suite 6E, 2333 Government St., Victoria, B.C. V8T 4P4, CANADA
Phone 250-383-6864 Toll-free 1-888-232-4444 (Canada & US)
Fax 250-383-6804 E-mail sales@trafford.com
Web site www.trafford.com TRAFFORD PUBLISHING IS A DIVISION OF TRAFFORD HOLDINGS LTD.
Trafford Catalogue #03-0900 www.trafford.com/robots/03-0900.html

10 9 8 7 6 5 4 3 2

In a direct way

This book is as much

Doctor Richard Kimble

as it is Dr. Dre.

In the end, I can say:

I am from them but I am not of them. I am not sick with seriousness. I do not have an ideal I want to attain. My life is silliness. I constantly seek approval. Even as I am disgruntled by denigrating words I say, "I deserve them." I tell myself "Roses have thorns," as I suck blood from my red fingers. I want to suffer from having journeyed. I want to wear a cloak of good fortune. I will cast it away later.

Tell me secretly, you love my work. Tell others you hate it. Help me achieve my goal. Tell me your criticism is an attempt to strengthen your fragile reputation. I want security amongst my peers. If you loathe me, I will be secure.

Remember: I not only seek your approval. I want it authenticated. What for? When I receive it all I can give you is an unappreciative, lackluster response.

Tell me you adore me. I will leave you with the impression your praise is hardly worth my time. I will leave you with the impression I am a man who avoids contact with people who are likely to dote on me. I am so comatose I am convinced I shall never hear a kind word directed towards me or my efforts again.

Publicly fault my work. It is a noble deed. Aspire towards nobility. Deride me. Make me a household name for being so worthy of disdain.

Infamy combined with record sales will provide a peaceful respite from your harsh, noble criticism.

Say something bad about what I've written to my face and I will deem you unworthy of judging me. Understand me clearly: I do not care what the public thinks. When I know you intimately I will lend your expert opinion the credence it deserves. Until then, only your praise merits my radar. This is something I am not eager to acknowledge.

Keep this question in mind: what is the relevance of the public you're going to make hate me? It stands in front of me in line at the grocery store. It keeps me sitting still in traffic.

It is always a single touch beyond the reach of my able hands. It is an intangible and fanciful notion. Resentment for the masses gives way to music for them.

I am not the masses. I am not the voice of any group. My voice cannot be replicated. It is a voice seeking disputation. I am the shiver sender. You are an intellectual in need of stimulation. I provide something similar to it. I write reams to justify your scorn. Never one word more. I give you reason for your intellectual awakening. Raise it.

You say you've seen this before. You dazzle me with names of precursors as if they daunt on me. Fool!

Am I going to praise anybody with similar passages attributed to them? I am the sole author of these words. There is no comparison. How do you entertain the notion?

I am the everlasting victor based upon what I have written right now. Do not refer to this classic as seminal. Refer to it as instant. The title will outlast the ideas, but what do titles and ideas matter to you?

What do you think, so far, my friend with the snooping eyes? Are you asking yourself why I have posted this account? Be patient. It will be revealed. I must warn you: it lacks fluidity.

When I am a venerable old man plagued by senility I will not remember why it was written. Nor should you. Loneliness is not a father.

I am:

Sitting in this laundromat/dim sum cafe located three blocks from my rent-controlled loft, resting my enormous body on a petite, fiberglass bench. After perusing the tidy, horrid photos of an outdated LIFE magazine and finishing the appetizer, I rise from the bench to fetch my newly washed garments. I stand in line to be rung up by the cashier behind an old woman with a severely curved spine and a paltry-cheap wig plopped on her head.

The cashier tells me, "That'll be $2.75 for the wash and three dollars even for the pot stickers."

I pay the tab, smile at the man, and leave for the boulevard.

The boulevard is a collection of human negligence.

Boulevards whizzing with melodies of human energy: shops selling handbags, cafes hocking coffee and sandwiches, men forgetting the local language parking cars, are pleasant to walk along. This one is comatose. Its sidewalks are littered with deteriorating, craggy-faced men who keep company with boastful cardboard signs telling the sad story of their lives. The windows of the stores that aren't broken or covered with boards beg for customers. The aluminum lamps lining the filthy cement walkways need bulbs that don't burn so solemnly as if they are ashamed to shine down upon the pock marks of the street. The clutter of paper debris masks the blunt, native grayness of the lampposts. The sight of the lamps is as disappointing as journeying to a distant forest and finding Mother Nature has torched it.

But Mother Nature, after converting a tree to ash, does not forbid the wind from introducing seedlings into the area, nor forbid the rain and soil from impregnating the seeds with wood and green. The matrons of a city are not permissive—their rules destroy boulevards. Absent the rules, the boulevard is palatable. The street is flanked with squatty buildings. Some faced with granite. Some with pink marble. Cement lions prowl around the entrance to one building on the corner of the block where I reside. The roof of another is affixed with gargoyles in the shape of flames. A wall surrounding the perimeter of another tells an entire tale through the medium of cut stone. One could gaze at the buildings for an entire day and not notice all accouterments.

The details of the buildings do not register in the minds of most people. Such folks keep the waywardness of their glances to a minimum to avoid getting mugged.

I do not fear muggers. I am such a lonely man the thought of any company at all is pleasant. I am large, polite and I don't have anything anybody wants. I tower above everybody. When I become immersed in my own sensibleness, I often fail to adequately duck my head for the purpose of passing through a doorway unscathed. For my thoughts, I have been graced with a bruise of a purple hue. I remember visiting a castle once. I did not duck my head there. That's another story.

I cannot permit myself to speak of my excursions. I bore people in person. If I bore you with this account it is your fault.

This is the nature of literature. My literary nature. If I bore or confuse you, you are inadequate, not me nor my incompetence. Pass along this account to someone more worthy of it than you.

My physical features:

I tell the people I meet personally I am only seven foot five. It baits them and I soon have a brief conversation to look forward to. "Oh, no, you must be five or six inches taller than that," they say. I exclaim, "No," but they're correct. I have green eyes, canon-shaped arms, a barrel chest, stout legs, and a thinning head of charcoal gray hair sitting on an olive-skinned scalp. [Permit me to use this space to thank the editors of my thesaurus for their diligence. Were it not for them I would have thinning green eyes, barrel shaped arms, a cannon-like chest, and olive skinned hair sitting atop a charcoal-gray scalp.]

I lie about my national origin. I do so benignly. I was adopted as a child. I know nothing of my birth parents. I rarely speak of my adoption.

I Think:

There is a shortage of politeness. I do not want humanity healed of this shortcoming. If the moral code of humanity is complete I add nothing to the lives of others. I have been lazy and apathetic and added little to the lives of anyone so far, so here I give you the first step I am taking towards fixing the planet (and taking it out for a spin).

I intend to enter a modern priesthood and absorb the arts of a religion deifying me: Literature. To honor the praise of my congregation, I plan to conceal every hateful thing about myself. I long to drape myself with badges and shawls of accomplishment. I detect desire within my enormous bones and bulky flesh. Desire is illuminated sometimes as images of the fictitious history and even more fictitious future of my fantasy life with a woman who, I'll bet, is sitting on her couch scolding her child right now, waiting for her husband to return home from work.

A reality such as this casts its shadow and then I am taken away by the brilliance of another.

Insipid commentary:

A woman I know represents every current indication of beauty. A tide of ecstasy is not socked through my veins when I look upon her though. When other men meet her, their pants and hearts go nutty. Desire for her is too common, making it detestable to this king of passions who will never hold court with a woman based on the carving of her bust.

Current Indication Dame has a companion with terrible posture, and a cacophonous voice. She is Woman-in-waiting. (Why am I writing this? So people can read it and assume these are my personal thoughts? So they can say, "Ah! Now there is a man who has discovered something" or, "Ah! Now there is a man who missed a target." I discover nothing. I am neither source, nor destination and certainly not anything in-between.) Woman-in-waiting assumes, by the fact she has been on this planet for thirty-five years, if the wrinkles under her eyes are any indication of age, she deserves something more in return than food, shelter, and other rudiments. You can see her desire, but not quite 'desire' because she feels she is 'owed' this for something great. I do not know what she did to create this great debt. (I have just stolen this line from another author. If you happen to know this author, you do not win a prize. So there! This is what you get for all that intellect). Woman-in-waiting is horrid looking. Her face isn't marred or striking. It is entirely forgettable.

I wouldn't spend more than a half-minute in conversation describing her face as it is so meritless. The only thing remarkable about her is the sloppiness of her posture.

A man I know irritates me for an abominable reason. I cannot effectively ridicule him. He does it himself. His self-deprecation encourages people to enjoy him. Except me. I find him benign, foolish, and naive. I loathe the way he obnoxiously updates his haircut every six weeks, but I cannot harp on him for this because he takes charge of poking fun at the money he spent on shampoos, dyes, and mousse. People remind him he's a delight to have around as he persists in pointing out how much money he's spent since he graduated college solely on his hair. Before you know it, someone is kissing him, tugging his cheek, calling him an irresistible sweety. Don't they notice he has wide hips like a woman and he wears his pants too low? Were his parents cartoonists? If I had the opportunity to become better friends with him I would decline. What need have I for being friends with him? Loneliness isn't that bad. Envisioning our friendship inside my mind for five minutes is all the friendliness I can muster for him. A minute longer than that and I am forced to protect myself with a shield of directed hypochondria: the thought of being friends with him makes me irreversibly nauseous and weakens me to the point at which I look upon the opportunity to vomit as the only possible remedy to the intestinal pain I suffer. I'm a giant baby who fears he will only top the growth charts.

The bookstore, managed by the cartoonists' son, serves coffee:

I see them at the bookstore frequently, Current Indication Dame and Woman-in-waiting. I have noticed a pattern to their frequent jaunts to the store. Current spends her time sorting through masses of publications dedicated to making women like her live happy, healthy lives. Woman-in-waiting retrieves a book from the philosophy section before settling down and drinking a cup of cafe au lait.

She reads the back cover in detail. She is, I am certain, looking to see who is suggesting she buy a book analyzing the "problem of meaning." She reads the back cover repeatedly to verify the names of the scholars or to place them more firmly in her memory. She pays close attention to the inside flaps of the cover (where a summary of the book is written). Between sips of coffee, she flips through the first couple of chapters. She reads five or ten pages of the book's midsection.

She scans the book to its end and reads the final paragraph with utmost intensity displayed in her face. She sets the book on the table and pumps more amperage of consternation to her grim looking mug (The one on her head, not the one sitting before her). Were anyone to catch a glimpse of her with the book, her face would suggest she is deeply provoked by its contents.

On this particular day, Woman-in-waiting sets the book on the edge of the table. As her younger companion, Current, is nowhere to be seen, I decide to take action.

Mesh-talk:

"Excuse me, I didn't mean to be so clumsy," I said as I fetched her book from the floor. "Are you an admirer of Mr. Heave-ho?"

Be patient friendly reader, I would gladly answer your question, "Why name him Mr. Heave-Ho?," but I accidentally deleted the explanation and I'm not entirely certain at this point whether you'll benefit from it or not. Chances are you will forget the explanation and then fail to remember you have forgotten it at which point you will supply your own explanation when you need to charm your friends as you discuss over cocktails that odd piece written with that lovable lout Heave-ho in mind.

"Heave-ho raises some very interesting questions regarding traditional dichotomies."

"Absolutely," I pretended to know what she was talking about.

"Binary systems of thought will always plague us." She said sipping her cafe au lait. "I can only sit here and espouse the truth of what I know." she paused, "Were written language not the product of a hierarchy striving to oppress Opinion-As-It-Lives, I would be fit to write my own book. I can't attain certitude through writing though. Language lives. As soon as a word is written the meaning changes, the author's entire attitude toward a work changes after it has been written. So whose work is it? Sure, one could argue it belongs to Heave-ho. It's his name on the cover. Who is he? His wife knows him as I do not. He is a professor. His students know him differently than his wife. When he lectures, his audience knows him differently at the end of the lecture than the beginning. Can anyone be wrong?" she paused, "Ultimately, language must indict itself for being transparent."

Damn! Damn! Damn! If she's correct, making friends will be a lot harder than originally anticipated.

She continued talking. She practiced her thesis to perfection. Her language was devoid of meaning. I couldn't avoid bumping the table, could I?

Upon reading a book of her choosing:

Utopians are not on the planet. They dedicate themselves to sounding either pious or scholarly to dull the bluntness of their message. The central theme of utopian thought is this: inner-peace in outer space.

Perhaps they will be happier living within the world when they dedicate more time to improving themselves and less time telling me where I can go and offering me a contraption to get me there.

Social critics who complain about the style of architecture in our cities have little, if any, influence upon architects. Their influence is upon others who want to whine about the imperfections which arise within the content of the material world (I forget from whom I stole this weighty gem. If you recognize it as one of yours get on the horn with your lawyer and haul me into court for plagiarism because this is the pinnacle of decent writing and I am not about to relinquish it.).

They do not truly want to have better buildings built. If they did, they would build them. Instead, they become parasites on the arms of creators and they are more ambiguous than the coffee-pouring cartoonist's son.

Of their work I can only think of the painter who uses oil colors to depict curved fruit, which appears deliciously edible, perhaps due to the drops of water flecked onto its skin, and could completely fool the observer into thinking it was really delicious if it weren't for the flatness of the canvas.

These opinions! What to make of them? I espouse these beliefs because I could not play soccer as a child, nor basketball. Hobbies bored me.

For example:

I had been sitting in a corner for a half-hour at a local bar when I was approached by a man of nondescript features. I was watching the other patrons yelling at any one of the seven televisions located throughout the crowded room airing a football game that had been locked in a tie for several minutes.

He said he visited the bar whenever he needed relief from his chosen craft of songwriting. He did not come here for drinks he assured me, merely to watch the other patrons. When he noticed me and saw how intent I was upon watching the other patrons, he decided to introduce himself. We engaged in polite yammering and before long, he asked if I knew about the surge.

I knew nothing about the surge.

The surge, according to his definition, was a label, albeit all labels are negations he added, which referred to an individual's ability to gain knowledge of its own self. He claimed it was imperceptible to detect. In his words, "Listen to this, my friend, when a couple of guys like you and I take a look at ourselves, and I'm not talking about staring in a mirror or something like that, I mean, when you and I really take a look at how our life has been lived, the things we've done, you know, the choices we've made. We, whether we know it or not, are searching for signs of the surge. We want to see something—ANYTHING—that says, "You, my friend, are connected to this world and to everybody in it; past, present, and future. "

The fact I didn't even know who my birth parents were didn't prevent me from playing along.

"A great poet," he continued, scooping a chunk of salsa with a tortilla chip from the bowl in front of us, "doesn't look at what he's written and say, 'That'll do.' No way, man. I'll tell you what he's doing: Every night, he's sitting up, wondering how his poem is going to fit into the whole scope of history. He thinks to himself, ‘What affect will this have upon the surge. Will it benefit or disturb the universe?’" The man paused for a moment and looked about the room with a disturbed scowl. It took me a moment to realize the salsa must have been too spicy. I motioned for the waitress to bring him a glass of water.

He regained his composure. He did not mention the potency of the salsa, his watery eyes and reddened complexion verified it irritated him.

"When a woman decides it's time to have a baby, do you really think she's thinking about nothing more than what its name will be and how her life will be after it's born? No way. You're way off, man. I'll tell you what she's thinking, She's thinking about the surge. What's this kid going to do in life? How's this kid going to affect the world? People think these things, my friend. More than you'd know." He paused as though I needed this thought to sink into my mind thoroughly to make room for some more of his insights. "She asks herself, What ne-ces-si-tates the birth of this child?"

I gathered he had acquaintance with some incredibly articulate people. The woman he spoke of was nothing like any of the technicians' wives I knew from the shop where I worked.

"People," he began, "do not know they think this. You know why? Most of them are stupid. They have their heads shoved way far up their asses. They don't know what they think. Half the time." He paused and smiled a satisfied grin. "That's the thing about this surge thing, you can't deny it. You can't ignore it. You may not know it's there. You may not look for it. You may forget you are a human being and the purpose of your life is living fully. But, when all is said and done, we're all human, and we are ALL products of the world. Anything we do here," He continued, "is the result of our having lived here. And that's it." He continued, "When you see a person deep in thought, they are proving the surge exists. Sure, it's all kind of tenuous, in a way. But, the time will come," he stated as though he was positioned to offer an unconditional guarantee, "when all of humanity will be unified."

He took the sopapilla and began eating it. I don't think it entered his mind commerce was responsible for bringing him the food of mine he was so diligently consuming.

"This is good shit," He paused and munched. And munched some more. "Yeah, all this fuck about jobs and being productive is a bunch of shit. People don't need jobs. They need to examine their lives. They need to realize where they fucked up. They need to see life is shit and you have to cope."

I did not understand why my having listened to him for this long gave him license to curse profusely. I hoped he didn't come from the class of people who are polite upon introduction and became successively more rude and more inconsiderate with each subsequent meeting. I am certain I am not of that ilk. My politeness is indelible.

"That's it! That's it." He seemed to make similar exclamations many times over half-silently as he continued to chomp the sopapilla, nodding repeatedly to let me know how much he was enjoying it. "We, through our superior faculties, show others how to live. We show them the truth of their existence."

The kind of overt self-praise he was wallowing in annoyed and greatly sickened me. I was prone to passionately hate anybody who had so little faith in my ability to lead my own life they felt compelled to force me to lead it otherwise.

When I was young I was free to make my own decisions. When I chose poorly, my ass would hear about it from the force of my father's hand.

I did not hate my parents. I was neither annoyed nor greatly sickened by them. I was their child. They raise. I rebel. I rise. They rebel.

The strength my parents had in teaching me how to live was not so forceful and oppressive I could not occasionally reject their rules. Other institutions are not so lax. They demand their rules be heeded. If they feel they have hastily overlooked someone's rebellion, the usually slow and laborious bureaucratic mechanism they operate within becomes a swift and fiery dragon torching the offender from behind.

The boy continued to speak a series of ironies greatly perplexing me. What he really needed was a beer, but he was a few years shy of qualifying for one of those.

He told me he wasn't a philosopher. He preferred to be called a musician entertaining philosophical thoughts. He resented philosophy. It is doomed to obscurity. An adequate position for his thinking. I was the only person he was entertaining and I didn't like what I was hearing.

Were the ideas of which he spoke destined for popularity, I am certain he would have found a different method of sustaining his loathing attitude. I cannot say the same thing for Philosophy. Socrates is more popular. Aristotle is less widely disputed. Popper. Hume. Drop name. Drop name. Drop name. Friedrich Hayek. Ludwig von Mises. Drop all synonyms. This account will impress your friends. Resist associations. Place it on your coffee table if you can.

He was a disdainful and fragile man. I asked him to keep his articulate hatred to himself. I hoped it would perish sooner than he would.

I was a shy man. I liked to keep to myself. I did not need lengthy diatribes upon society to explain why I remained alone. A short one would do.

I was also a strong man. I rarely contemplated weakness because I wanted nothing to do with it. A person with restraint and discipline is always admirable.

One of my occasional bouts of sentimentality:

As a child, I often looked to my parents for guidance. I wanted to be esteemed by them. I have too many memories of them telling me how wonderful the neighbor's children were though. I never disagreed with my parent's assessment of the neighbor's children until I spent an entire spring afternoon playing hide and seek with them.

I had not realized, until the second round, the other two boys secretly decided to hide in secluded areas so the girl—who was *it*, might, upon finding them, let them press their lips against hers and rub her breasts which were growing larger with each passing day with their hands which were more accustomed to maneuvering toy trucks over bumpy terrain.

The memory of their erotic play haunted me for a long time. Now, I again see the same charm of the game as I did when I was playing it. I thought the girl would be offended by the game. I was wrong. She enjoyed it.

The boys enjoyed it. I also wanted to enjoy it, but the boys excluded me from participating.

To combat my exclusion from their naughtiness, I stripped off my clothing and squatted on home base resting my arms around my gangling legs until they finished their game. When the trio returned to the rock, the fanciful smiles on the boys, which were fueled by the girl's kisses, were replaced with gaping wide-eyed expressions of fear and embarrassment at my complete nudity. The girl stood intrigued. Her smile found a new source of fuel—me. She took my nudity as a dare and stripped off her clothing.

We did not say anything. We examined each other with our eyes. But we never came closer than a few feet from each other. I couldn't smell her. I was so consumed with the naked girl I did not notice the boys had disappeared. The vision of her lovely awkwardness is still with me.

Her shoulders and knees were bony. A little fat to pad them would have made them beautiful. Her brown nipples were swollen, making her breasts look like they were growing according to the shape of the nipple the way a pup grows according to the size of its paw. Hair was just beginning to grow on her snatch. She and I were changing, but nothing was changing in our direction.

If I met this girl again the only question I would ask her is whether her fascination with me equaled mine with her. I fear what her answer might be so I am thankful I never see a face resembling hers on the boulevard.

The boys had taken it upon themselves to tell their parents the girl and I were busy hitting a 'home run' on home base. Sure enough, as she and I stood gazing at each other, four sets of parents filed into the woods to see us dressed as elegantly as the day we were born. Their expressions were not immediately those of parents about to scold their children.

I insist they were delighted in finding us. I also insist they would have been disappointed had they traveled the entire fifty yards into the woods and found us otherwise.

There was grandness in this tale for them. A departure from the usual, petty, deviousness of children. This tested the limits of their parenting skills, justifying the raise-a-happy-honor-student books they purchased.

I do not resent the boys for telling the parents. I wish the folks walked slower to the woods. A LOT slower. The tykes reported our actions as if there was severe wrongdoing on our part. They resented me for having broken the rules of their game and attracted the girl in a more favorable way.

I have always broken the rules ever since then, not loudly, mind you. I have only done so in the silent, meaningless swarm of
my own mind.

My rebellion no longer serves me well. It aggravates my desire to embrace plainness and live fully within the confines of commonness. I lied earlier about wanting to be different from my peers. I did so with good intent. Had I plainly told you of my desire to cultivate commonplace values and of my desire to schedule my day according to the television guide, you surely would have laid this manuscript to rest. A fragile person like you, so in need of something vigorous and unfamiliar, must be extremely thankful for my courteous deception. I will become a part of the public I loathe so much I claim it does not exist. I scoff away those who deride it.

Intimacy:

Everybody shares an infallible connection with their best friend's spouse. And sometimes not. Tell me secretly about the daily composition of your life. Did you feel resentment today? I did too. Think of what you are truly married too. Is it that person snoring beside you in bed? I will say you are bound to something greater. Something vague and unspeakable. We all are. Did you encounter someone who treated you rudely today? So did I. Did it disturb your spouse? It did mine. How silly of me to continue this stupid contrivance! We cannot divorce ourselves from our existence or anyone else's.

Yet the horror of life is so much more palatable when it is presented as something tangible sitting on a buffet of metaphors (How cute! I shall reach around and scratch my back for my cuteness). We have all been treated rudely yet there are many whom, upon being treated this way, seem to think it affects them more severely than it affects durable and resilient people like you and me. Listen, I will try and relate a story fitting the mold I have cast. If it is a poor fit I promise to provide you with plenty of excuses for its inconvenient size, otherwise you may not tell your friends how truly awful I am for bringing this account to you.

Trashy plot:

I was once asked by a friend, a man whom I did not know very well, if I would join him on a double-date. He said a woman he was attracted to would dine with him provided he brings a date for her best friend. He said he chose me because I was polite. When he called, he noted my good nature and height already provided a wonderful icebreaker. I was a toy. No doubt, I was not the first toy on his list of possible candidates.

I met the man at his apartment. Our only similarity was the cologne he took the liberty of spraying on me because, as he said in a tone specifically intended to highlight a discernable and prolific funkiness, "It drives hooches wild."

We drove to the apartment of the woman to whom he was attracted. Upon meeting her, I noticed nothing but her innocence—her non-smoking naiveté. I no longer wondered why he was so compelled by her.

He couldn't handle a fully-grown woman who had seen the world through her own eyes. He belonged to the class of men who longed to be a pair of pleasantly tinted spectacles they could place on the dainty nose of a dame. His date reminded me of the little girl on the rock but, as the little girl was awestruck by the world, it was quite obvious this woman was selectively blind to it.

This selective blindness, you understand, allowed her to continue to flatter her existence unmolested by sharp-tongued mongrels like myself.

My friend's charm (If only I had a more fitting term for him—Ah! Why don't I call him Hog Bog?) was worn like a suit of armor. *You can't hurt me, I'm charming.* It was just as clumsy and clunky and, all the same, magnificent, because he could maneuver diligently inside of it.

The All-grown-up-little-girl had a best friend who was blandly overweight. If my date was going to be overweight, the best I could hope for was someone fat in a remarkable way. The ploppiness of this woman was plain and dull the way an enormous boiled potato might be given her face.

Upon my entering, she smiled a well-rehearsed grin and grunted her salutation in a voice which was, at the same time, both pinched and husky.

The pinched sound was due no doubt to the pinched shape of her nose. The huskiness I attributed to the dour roast of cigarettes hanging above her. She was clearly using her attire as a device to convince people she was petite.

The restaurant was a fun-bar called Passengers Come As You Are. The employees were dressed as aviators and railroad workers; a few were even dressed as bus drivers.

Such cuteness in commerce! It catered to men who knew whether their boots should be pointed or blunt at the toe and women who knew what length their skirt should be according to a standard that would change in a week.

All-grown-up spoke as though she were peeling an onion--each new topic of conversation yielding a less superficial take on things. She switched topics in mid-air and repeated herself constantly. She applied to the art of conversation the same rules applying to jazz improvisation. Not precisely. I'm not skilled in the art of jazz improvisation, and she didn't have room for a clarinet in her mouth.

My chubby sour-faced companion gave me the silent treatment during the car ride and at the restaurant. When the waitress came, she ordered only a salad. "Who are you kidding?" I wanted to ask. I knew she had an appetite requiring truckloads of food to satisfy.

Hog Bog was a chart-topper that evening. He managed to bring so many varied aspects of his personality to light all the while spending a considerable amount of time listening to All-grown-up go on and on convincing us of her genuine worldliness.

I attempted once again to converse with my chubby companion. I wanted to ease her out of her nervousness. But she just ignored me. I found myself sitting among a group of people amidst a roomful of even more people—all of whom were there for the sole purpose of socializing, and I found myself suffering from loneliness. Not having anyone to talk to caused me to yearn for my dreary apartment from which I so often longed to be free.

I was so in need of a familiar voice I excused myself from the table and called home so I could hear the sound of my own voice on the outgoing message of my answering machine. I didn't expect to hear anyone else's, but it was worth a shot.

When I returned to the table, I asked my chubby companion if something bothered her. I was eager to listen. She soon became defensive and asked if I had some greater expectation from her for the evening. My friend and All-grown-up were so involved in showcasing themselves they didn't notice Chubby's and my exchange. I told her I had no expectations for the evening. I should have just told her she was ugly enough to fuck.

She folded her arms. She was mad at me because I wasn't going to give her the chance to turn me down. She asked, "How do you want me to act?"

I looked at her blankly as if the thought of being upbeat and conversational required regulatory oversight. I'd accept surly behavior from someone I wanted to dive on top of, but I was not about to accept it from someone I had so little interest in that she had to compete with my answering machine for my attention. Didn't she realize what a massive departure this was for me? Didn't she realize how accustomed I had become to…what does it matter? She didn't know how to act.

I flirted with the waitress for lack of something better to do. I wanted to know more than her name.

I wanted to wallow in her spunkiness. What more could I desire than to linger forever in the presence of another human being? My company at the table did not attempt to thwart my efforts to flirt with her, but they clearly did not appreciate it. She was, after all, our server. She was utterly pleasing.

The pleasure she gave me was heightened by the fact I never expected to meet her. Yet, having met her, I was propelled to a state of bliss. A state I would never propel myself to alone.

Chubby was as disgruntled by my friendliness towards the waitress as she was disgruntled by seemingly everything existing within time and space, with the exception of the potato skins I ordered.

Let her be disgruntled, there was no way I was going to be friendly to her. Especially not when meanness is the backbone to lucrative book contracts. I could not compete with her on that field. She started speaking. As she spoke of that which she loathed, I thought of all of the things I hated. I hated being bombarded with information regarding sexually transmitted diseases which, when scrutinized, seemed to be the product of a scare monger's desire stir up panic and not the result of rigorous scientific and medical examination.

Many will believe all they can about disease, when all they know about it came from some doctor.

I want to fight a war so I can hate that too.

If I fight a war and continue to live perhaps I can become a hero. I can be decorated with medals and hang plaques on my walls. I am doing that already. Inside my mind.

The highest thing a person can value is the ability of their own self: their ability to transform their energy into an activity, which will withdraw the very best energy from a fellow human being. The trophy displayed on the wall of a track runner is a good example. It is more than a combination of finished wood and ornate medal. It is a small representation of physical supremacy. It stands not as a monument to be praised forever, but as an obstacle waiting to be replaced by someone of an even greater physical prowess.

So where is my trophy for my physical prowess? These fingers deserve something for all I put them through night after night—special recognition is deserved for my deft use of 'Backspace' and 'Delete'.

To return to my chubby companion: She had just as long a hate list as I. I kept mine silent. I was glad to note she and I had absolutely nothing in common we despised. The opposition of a common enemy strengthens the most solid of all friendships. Nothing new here, so put away that bright, yellow marker. I was also glad to note her lethargy. It meant I wouldn't have to compete with her on the Bestseller list as angriest author.

The close of our date, upon returning to All-grown-up's apartment, created the first awkward moment of the evening for all of us. A moment in which plain speech among the participants would have been a social no-no. A common moment. I'll share it with you:

Since Hog Bog drove me to All-grown-up's apartment, I was in need of a ride home. Chubby, clearly disgruntled by my, and many other men's, lack of interest in her, was ready to open the floodgates in All-grown-up's apartment. Her desire conflicted with All-grown-up's desire to hump Hog Bog. Hog Bog was unaware if I knew of his desire to practice legally sanctioned pedophilia for the rest of the evening.

If I was unaware, I would need him to drive me home and his plans would be thwarted. Neither Hog Bog nor All-grown-up were dumb enough to ask Chubby to drive me home. Plain speech would have permitted All-grown-up to say (Were she witty, which she is not, so I'll just have to assert my artistic certification here), "Chubby, you'll have to catch a later flight for the pity-trip you have planned, I have some fucking to tend to." (Go ahead, reread it. Appreciate it. You know it took me three minutes to compose that sentence!)

Hog Bog would not need to say anything to me. I'm always hip to two people who want to hump and I am never inclined to mount an opposition.

I let the awkwardness of the moment linger in the room before I announced I was up to the task of walking home. My friend and his prospective hump-mate made the requisite "Oh, no, it's too far." statement. To which I responded, "Not for me. I have long legs."

The walk home was successful. I passed many wanderers including a group of intimidating looking boys. I wondered if they would try and attack me for the novelty of tumbling a giant. They just passed by though. Lonely little me. Suspense and adventure no longer require conquering virgin frontier. A late night walk in a well-regulated city suffices. Men retire their cardboard signs by sundown and approach passersby directly, "Do you have any change?" They ask.

All I want to do is plead with them to understand I am the carrier of the unwavering traditions of the eagerly willing and of the intellectual landfill solicitors. Before I can finish my sentence, they make it clear they suddenly don't even want my pocket change.

During the daytime, I belong to a laboring class of men noted mostly for their fondness of sporting events and the hardiness of imported beer. They eagerly await new things to be produced so they may enjoy and conquer them. They sustain themselves on modest incomes allowing them to accrue new gadgets as they are marketed. At night time, as I plunk away, I solicit books and people for space in a vast, velvet landfill. A throw down of notions.

Solicitors have plenty of ideas of their own but are more concerned with trashing others. They also want to keep their own ideas far from the landfill. Being a part of the solicitor class is more seductive than being a member of the eagerly willing because it is both despicable and clever. Clever because it constantly redefines mockery. Despicable because the cruelty of the mockery is fully intended and only partially revealed. Most solicitors seek refuge from the eagerly willing because of their failure to see the causal connection between what occurs in reality (That area which, according to human perception, seems to remain undaunted by it) and how it conflicts with the dogmatic tone of their suppositions.

Many solicitors, even those as proudly dogmatic as myself, are prone to making this claim:

I claim publicly I am not attempting to hasten the popularity of a belief. I regard my work as though writing it required the diligence of a tightrope walker because I am such a keen observer of my tendency to seek familiarity and give preference to the friendly.

Such larceny! I am a thief of notions. The words I have written here are more eloquent in their original form. I have absconded with another's ideas and fashioned them to my liking.

Now you ask: How thankful am I for privacy? Without it I would be a complete fraud.

Speaking of fraud:

Recently, I discovered a plan some co-workers devised to embezzle money. The details of the plan will not be divulged because it is so clever and so readily applicable to other professions I would, no doubt, be held accountable for subsequent copycat crimes.

I can see myself sitting in a court of law behind a wooden table. You are sitting to my left at another table. There are many television cameras filming, not a court proceeding, but an event. Next to you sits your lawyer and the wife of a prominent politician. She, and many others, is convinced the crime of which you are accused is not the product of your own doing but the result of having been tempted by the account of a well-crafted scheme I provided you via this manuscript. No such luck.

I was smart enough to know better than to ditch 20s from the cash drawer at my teenage pizza joint, but that doesn't mean I wasn't splitting free cash with the cooks through some other means.

I have been employed at the computer repair company longer than anyone else. Hence, I am the only supervisor. I was not supposed to know about the plan concocted by the other employees because I would be likely to report it to the owner who infrequently checks on the business personally. The plan involves altering invoices after they have been processed. However, unbeknownst to the other employees, the plan ultimately fails because I bored myself silly a long time ago writing scripts essentially fraud-proofing the system through excruciatingly detailed log file analysis.

I wish I could say my own hearty diligence was responsible for discovering the plan. However, I am not heroic, nor cunning, nor wise. I checked my mailbox one afternoon to find my mailer worked better than expected. I have to hand it to my co-workers; they just about reinvented the wheel for an extra few every week. Foolproof. Not rhythm proof. What tipped me off wasn't the plan itself, but this absurd suite I put together tracking people's login routines. They all logged in after hours (some remotely), and accessed the central order system with write-access. All for approximately the same amount of time.

The significance of the crime:

All my life I have wanted to belong. Yet, I am ashamed to admit the group I sought connection with has always rejected me. I write this manuscript because it allows me to deride those I seek before they degrade me. Most people find plenty of reasons for hating me. Most of their reasons are childish and rude. Reasons that should be reserved for the playground.

As old as I am, I have yet to cease yearning to be included and recognized as a member, perhaps a leader, of something meaningful. In the bosom of company there is solitude. In my apartment there is only loneliness, and a cat.

The discovery of my co-worker's deviousness presented me two options. I could join them in their fraudulent scheme and enjoy full membership to their club which, although it didn't exist officially, would allow me to drink with them on Fridays, ball games on Saturday, barbecue on Sunday, and augment my monthly income with my share of the loot. Or, I could tell the owner of the company about the plan in such a way that would earn me his respect as a person. He already respected me as an employee.

I did not want to choose the first option. I knew the life of my co-workers too well. Naturally, I did no want to be like them.

The owner:

A wealthy man living in a beautiful home.

He was the sole owner of the computer repair shop, which he often considered selling, and had accrued a fortune by investing in other business ventures. I decided to inform him in person.

I rode the bus to the bus stop nearest his home on a warm Sunday afternoon. I never purchased a car of my own because Monday through Friday I was free to use the company truck. On weekends I stayed indoors typing this manuscript most of which I have failed to provide here because I fear you might rely on it to ensure your good night's rest.

I walked the short distance from the bus stop to his house. The sun was hot causing me to sweat profusely, staining the back of my shirt, and leaving stains under my arms. Although I dressed properly for the occasion, I feared my sweat would impair the image I was trying to present to the owner.

I knew my clothing would be acceptable because I purchased the same outfit Hog Bog had worn only in a much larger size. It was casual but not without an air of glamorousness.

I approached the door. I could hear the sound of people enjoying themselves in the backyard. The door opened. The maid greeted me. I met her previously. She led me to the back of the house where the guests gathered around the black-bottomed pool.

I walked onto the patio and was promptly greeted by the owner who had been standing next to a bar speaking in his usual gregarious manner to two other men. He shook my hand firmly and smiled and introduced me as the manager of the firm. I was surprised by his kindness because, although I ran the place, my salary was not much higher than the other employees, I had never been given an official title, and I was certain he preferred the humor and general nature of some of the other employees to my own.

He asked me to explain how the firm was run and how it became profitable to the other men.

I explained how the shop operated but stayed cautious because I have a bad habit of losing people's interest when I tell a story. Most people simply are not interested in what I have to say. Even I would rather be outside of myself and immersed in a football game, but I have a terrible throwing arm, I can't tackle, and I have an aversion to physical pain. The men were interested by my remarks and even asked questions. I was not at all accustomed to the undivided of the attention of the three men.

I expected them to be searching for ways to politely exit the conversation either by refilling their drinks or finding somebody whom they 'needed' to talk to.

However, they continued to listen to me. I decided this was the best time to mention I knew the business so well I had personally discovered a sinister plot by the other employees to embezzle from the company.

My announcement came as a surprise to each of the men and it was, upon my telling them this fact I lost the attention of the two guests to whom I had just been introduced.

The duo promptly excused themselves leaving me to gaze down at my short boss who suddenly appeared angry.

He stared at me in confusion.

"Why didn't you mention this before?" He asked restraining his frustration with me.

I told him I had informed him of the plot as soon as I discovered it. I asked if he wanted to know the details of the plan. He declined to listen and told me the men to whom I had been talking were potential investors interested in buying the business. Apparently, my comment thwarted the sale of the business.

I asked him why he was interested in selling a business, earning a modest profit and ready for growth. He merely said he had other plans.

My boss did not tell me to leave but he made it quite clear I would be wise to do so. I did not think I jeopardized my job because my boss seemed to always regard my social grace, despite my proficiency at running the business, as something of a burden.

I was angry with myself to the point of tears. Almost to the point of tears.

Upon entering the house I envisioned myself living there. I wanted the people to be my friends. I wanted the caterers to wait for me at the end of the evening so I could pay them. I wanted everything he had. Except, perhaps, I would place a library in the room in which he housed a giant television.

As I walked down the street, tears fell from my cheeks. I failed.

Do not feel sorry for me. Two days later I was more than reconciled with my hurt feelings.

The Monday following my having divulged the plan to the owner was a somber occasion. The owner had written a letter and photocopied one duplicate for each employee. It was a simple letter.

It read:

If you want to keep your job, don't do anything to get you fired. If you have any doubts about the merit of your actions, consult manager.

Everyone agreed he could be talking about no one else but me.

All seven of the workers were familiar with the owner's trite and vague style of management. We knew to what the letter referred. No one suspected me of having said anything.

I was grateful the owner didn't do anything causing friction between the others and me.

The following day I fully overcame my hurt feelings. The six other employees walked around the business as if the floor was blanketed with pins, needles, and chipped glass.

I was now officially their manager, so they werc particularly careful with me. I was treated with respect. They had deliberately done wrong and now they were haunted by their wrongdoing. I reveled in their fear as I watched them adhere to a strict policy of good behavior.

Bawd:

To celebrate my having won the respect and ears of my co-workers I spent an entire evening at the disposal of two whores; an endeavor so expensive the memory of standing aimlessly in the aisle of the supermarket waiting for my mother to calculate the best price on canned goods must have slipped my mind.

One whore was blonde. Her breasts were larger than those of the other by a couple of handfuls. The other whore was brunette.

I feared my neighbors might hear my meanderings with my companions so I tried to keep the volume as low as possible. I will, someday, have a reputation to uphold.

The thought of anybody finding the company I was keeping propelled me to an extreme state of nervousness.

My nervousness triggered sweat from my forehead, neck, underarms, crotch, and back. I became deeply agitated. Heat from inside me ran along my spine flashed onto my cheeks and warmed my scalp. I decided to not let it inhibit me. I had paid too much money for their services.

Thinking of what clever remarks the sluts might make regarding the pungent odor of my body, forced a vision upon me. An epiphany of the most necessary kind.

My final offering to you:

As a result of my size, I was prone to having offensive body odor. Knowledge of this hideous aspect of myself did not prevent me from being enraged by the thought of these sluts noticing it. I stood up, towering over my computer in a fit of anger. I ejected the compact disk from the drive and pitched it against the wall with immense force.

The sluts I brought home were the software kind. I did not get them from the boulevard, but from a shop along the boulevard.

An elaborate anger brewed within me as I thought what message might have been personally recorded for me by the whores. "Take a shower! Use deodorant! See a doctor!" I heard them announce in their regular perky vigorous tones.

I detailed the life of woman-in-waiting so well after only having seen her enter a restaurant with two companions whom I did not know either. Why couldn't her voice have been the ephiphanal one? I'm willing to bet had I truly argued with the philosopher-musician in a restaurant and not on-line, I would have found someone direct enough to counsel me to seek help for my embarrassing condition. Yet, it was my embarrassing condition keeping the philosician and All-grown-up and all the others away from me.

It was my keen capacity for abstract thought allowing me to color the lives of everybody I have ever mentioned in this account and pass the nights undisturbed by their chatter and ignorant of any words of advice they may have given me regarding my condition.

I sat in my chair numb. I thought of this manuscript and realized the phrasing, the clever and impersonal names I had given its people, and the feigned sense of intimacy I created with readers—friends, I wished the readers were my friends—had not been the product of my own wise efforts to produce a readable and enjoyable account of one man's life and his disdain for the world.

It was the indirect result of a faulty nose and a love for eating garlic toast, and choosing helplessness as the means by which to quell my embarrassment. My giant tribute to the world of ideas driven by a bad case of B.O.!

Epilogue:

I made an appointment with a doctor. He said some medication and some other treatments could solve my problem. Most of all, he said I needed sweaty exercise. At 3:15 on Wednesday the 19th, my literary career came to an end.

I looked at myself in the mirror in the examination room. Visions of my excursions whipped through my head as they had done every night on the monitor before me. From this angle, I could see what I truly wanted: to be common and likable. I returned to the boulevard, slamming my head against the doorjamb along the way.